THE BROTHERS GRIMM

HANSEL AND GRETEL

ILLUSTRATED BY LISBETH ZWERGER

THE BROTHERS GRIMM

HANSEL AND GRETEL

ILLUSTRATED BY LISBETH ZWERGER
TRANSLATED BY ELIZABETH D. CRAWFORD

SCHOLASTIC INC.
NEW YORK TORONTO LONDON AUCKLAND SYDNEY

THE BROTHERS GRIMM

HANSEL AND GRETEL

ILLUSTRATED BY LISBETH ZWERGER, TRANSLATED BY ELIZABETH D. CRAWFORD

Beside a great forest there once lived a poor woodcutter with his wife and two children, a boy named Hansel and a girl, Gretel. In the best of times they had little enough to eat, but when famine came to the land, the man could no longer provide their daily bread.

One night, as he lay in bed tossing with worry, he sighed and said to his wife, "What is to become of us? How can we feed our poor children when we have no more for ourselves?"

"You know what, husband," replied his wife, "tomorrow morning early we will take the children into the forest and give them each a morsel of bread. Then we will go to our work and leave them alone. They will never find the way home again, and we will be rid of them."

"No, wife," said the man. "I will not do that. How could I bring myself to leave my children alone in the forest? Wild animals would soon come and tear them to pieces."

"Oh, you fool!" said she. "Then we must all four die of hunger. You may as well begin planing the planks for the coffins." And she left him no peace until at last he gave in.

"But I grieve for my poor children," said the man.

The two children had not been able to sleep for hunger and heard what their stepmother had said to their father. Gretel began to weep bitterly. "Now we are finished," she said to Hansel.

"Be quiet, Gretel," said Hansel. "Don't cry. I will save us."

Once their parents were asleep, Hansel got up, put on his jacket, opened the door, and slipped outside. The moon shone brightly, and the white pebbles that lay in front of the house gleamed like coins of pure silver. Hansel bent down and put as many into his coat pocket as it would hold. Then he went back inside.

"Be of good cheer, dear little sister, and sleep well," he said to Gretel as he lay down to sleep again. "God will not forsake us."

At break of day, even before the sun had risen, the woman came and wakened both children. "Get up, you lazy things! We are going into the forest to gather wood." Then she gave them each a small piece of bread and said, "There! You have something for lunch, but don't eat it beforehand. You will get no more."

Gretel put the bread under her apron, because Hansel had the stones in his pocket. Then they all took the path that led into the forest. They had gone only a little way when Hansel stopped and looked back at their house, and he did so again and again.

The father said, "Hansel, what are you standing there looking at? Take care you don't get left behind."

"Oh, Father," said Hansel, "I'm looking at my white kitten, who is sitting up on the roof to say good-bye to me."

"Fool," said the woman, "that isn't your kitten. It's only the morning sun shining on the chimney."

But Hansel had not been looking at the kitten. Rather, each time he stopped he had thrown one of the shining white pebbles from his pocket onto the path.

When they came to the middle of the forest, their father said, "Now, children, gather some wood. I'll build you a fire so you don't freeze."

Hansel and Gretel gathered a small mountain of brushwood. The fire was lit, and when the flames were burning high, the woman said, "Lie down by the fire, children, and rest. We are going deeper into the forest to cut wood. When we are finished, we will come back and fetch you."

Hansel and Gretel sat by the fire, and at noontime they ate their morsels of bread. They heard the blows of an axe and believed their father was nearby. But what they heard was not the axe. It was a branch he had tied to a dead tree so that the wind would swing it back and forth. After they had sat for a long time, their eyes closed with weariness and they fell sound asleep. When they finally awoke, it had grown dark. Gretel began to weep. "How shall we ever find our way out of the forest?" she cried.

But Hansel comforted her. "Just wait a little while, until the moon rises. Then we will certainly find the way."

Sure enough, when the full moon rose, Hansel took his little sister by the hand and followed the pebbles, which shimmered like coins of pure silver and showed them the way. They walked all through the night and came to their father's house at daybreak. They knocked at the door, and when the woman opened it and saw Hansel and Gretel, she said, "Oh, you bad children! Why did you sleep so long in the forest? We thought you were never coming back at all!"

Their father rejoiced, for leaving them behind all alone had wrung his heart.

Not long after there was again famine everywhere, and in bed at night the children heard the stepmother say to the father, "The food is all gone again. We have half a loaf of bread, and then we're done for. The children must go. We'll lead them farther into the forest, so they cannot find the way home again. Otherwise there's no hope for us."

The idea distressed the man, and he thought, It would be better for you to share the last mouthful with your children.

But the woman paid no heed to what he said and nagged him and reproached him. Once you've said yes, it's hard to say no, and because he had given in the first time, he gave in the second time too.

The children were still awake and listened to the argument. After the parents were asleep, Hansel got up to go and gather pebbles as he had done the time before. But the woman had locked the door, and Hansel couldn't get out. However, he reassured his little sister and said, "Don't cry, Gretel, and sleep well. God will surely help us."

Early in the morning the woman came and got the children out of bed. They received their pieces of bread, which were even smaller than the time before. Along the way Hansel crumbled his bread in his pocket, stopped every now and again, and dropped a crumb on the ground.

"Hansel," said his father, "why are you standing there looking around? Come along."

"I'm looking at my little dove, who is sitting on the roof to say good-bye to me," answered Hansel.

"Fool," said the woman, "that isn't your dove. It's the morning sun shining on the chimney."

But bit by bit Hansel threw all the crumbs on the path.

The woman led the children deeper into the forest than they had ever been in their lives. There again a huge fire was kindled, and the stepmother said, "Just sit there, children, and if you are tired you can sleep a little. We are going farther into the forest to cut wood, and in the evening, when we are done, we will come and fetch you."
When it was noon, Gretel divided her bread with Hansel, who had thrown all his on the path. Then they went to sleep. Evening fell and deepened, but no one came for the poor children.

They finally awoke to black night. Hansel comforted his little sister, saying, "Just wait until the moon comes up, Gretel. Then we'll see the breadcrumbs I dropped, and they'll show us the way home."
When the moon appeared, they got up. But the breadcrumbs were gone, for the many thousands of birds of the field and forest had picked them all up. "We will find the way all the same," said Hansel to Gretel, but they did not. They walked the whole night and the next day from morning till evening, but they did not come out of the forest. And they were still hungry, for they had eaten nothing but the few berries they found on the ground. They were so tired that their legs would no longer carry them, so they lay down under a tree and fell asleep.

Now it was the third morning since they had left their father's house. They began to walk again, but they kept going deeper into the forest. If help did not come soon, they would surely perish. At midday they saw a lovely little snow-white bird sitting on a branch. It sang so beautifully that they stood still to listen to it.

When the bird had finished, it spread its wings and flew off ahead of them. They followed it, until at last they came to a cottage where it perched on the roof. When Hansel and Gretel came closer, they saw that the cottage was made of bread and roofed with cakes, and the windows were of pure sugar. "We'll go and have ourselves a feast," said Hansel. "I want a piece of the roof, Gretel, and you can have some of the window. That should taste sweet." Hansel reached up and broke off a little of the roof, to see how he liked it, and Gretel went up to a window and nibbled on it. All at once a gentle voice called from inside:

"Nibble, nibble, munch, munch.
Who is gnawing on my house?"

The children answered:

"The wind, the wind,
The heavenly wind."

And they went right on eating, without pausing at all.
Hansel found the roof tasted very good and tore down a big piece of it, and Gretel poked out a whole windowpane and sat down to enjoy it.
Suddenly the door opened and out crept an old woman. She looked as old as the hills and supported herself on a crutch. Hansel and Gretel were so frightened that they dropped what they held in their hands.

But the old woman shook her head and said, "Oh, my dear children! Whoever brought you here? Come in and stay with me. No harm will come to you."

She took them by the hand and led them into her cottage. There she served them a good meal: milk and pancakes, with sugar, apples, and nuts. Afterwards two snowy little beds were made up, and Hansel and Gretel lay down in them and felt as if they were in heaven.

But the old woman only pretended to be so kind. She was a wicked witch, who lay in wait for children, and she had built her cottage of sweets so as to entice them thither. Whenever a child came into her power, she killed it, cooked it, and ate it, making a feast out of it. Witches have red eyes and cannot see well, but they have a good sense of smell, like animals, and can tell if people are near. When Hansel and Gretel had come into her part of the forest, she laughed wickedly and chortled, "I have them, and they shall not slip away from me."

Early next morning she arose before the children were awake, and when she looked at them both lying there so peacefully with their full pink cheeks, she murmured to herself, "They will make a tasty morsel."

Then she seized Hansel in her skinny hand and dragged him out to the yard, to a small kennel with a barred door, and shut him in. Cry as he would, she did not let him out. Next she went to Gretel and shook her awake. "Get up, lazybones!" she cried. "Fetch water and cook something good for your brother, who is outside in the kennel to be fattened. When he is fat enough, I will eat him."

Gretel began to cry bitterly, but it was fruitless. She had to do what the wicked witch demanded.

Now the best food was cooked for poor Hansel, but Gretel got only scraps. Each morning the old witch crept out to the kennel and called "Hansel! Stick out your finger so that I can feel how fat it is."

Instead, Hansel held out a small bone. With her dim eyes, the old witch could not see it and thought it was Hansel's finger. She marveled that he didn't grow fat at all. When four weeks had passed and Hansel was still thin, she was overcome with impatience and would wait no longer.

"Ho there, Gretel!" she called to the girl. "Hurry up and get water. Whether Hansel is fat or whether he's thin, tomorrow I will kill him and cook him."

Poor Gretel sobbed as she carried the water, and the tears streamed down her cheeks. "Dear God, help us!" she exclaimed. "If only the wild animals in the forest had eaten us, at least we would have died together."

"Save your bawling," said the old witch. "It will do you no good."

Early in the morning Gretel had to go out, hang the kettle of water on the fire, and light it.

"First we will bake," said the witch. "I've heated the oven already and kneaded the dough." She pushed poor Gretel toward the oven, which already had tongues of flame shooting from it.

"Crawl in," said the witch, "and see if it's hot enough for us to put the bread inside."

She intended to close the oven when Gretel was inside, and when she was roasted, the witch would eat her too. But Gretel guessed what she had in mind and said, "I can't do it. How can I get in there?"

"Silly goose," said the old witch, "the opening is big enough. Look now, I can even get in myself."

She hobbled forward and stuck her head in the oven. Then Gretel gave her a hard push so that she fell inside, slammed the iron door, and slid the bolt. The witch began to howl dreadfully, but Gretel ran away, and the wicked witch was burned to death.

Gretel ran straight to Hansel, opened his kennel, and cried, "Hansel! We are free! The old witch is dead!" And Hansel sprang out like a bird from its cage when the door is opened for it. How they did rejoice! They hugged each other, they danced about, they kissed each other. And then, because there was no longer anything to be afraid of, they went into the witch's house hand in hand. In every corner there were chests with pearls and precious stones inside.

"They are even better than pebbles," said Hansel, and he filled his pockets with as many as they would hold.

"I want to take some home, too," said Gretel, and she filled her apron full.

"But now, we should go," said Hansel, "so we can escape this witch's forest." They had walked only a few hours when they came to a huge lake. "We can't get across," said Hansel. "I can't see any road or footbridge." "There's no boat, either," said Gretel, "but there's a white duck. If I ask her, she'll help us across." Then she called:

> "Duckling, duckling,
> Help Hansel and Gretel.
> There's no footbridge and no track.
> Take us on your little white back."

The duckling came up, and Hansel seated himself and told Gretel to sit beside him.

"No," answered Gretel. "We'll be too heavy for the little duck. She must take us one after the other." The good little creature did so, and after they were safely across and had gone on for a while, the forest began to look more and more familiar to them. Finally, from a distance, they recognized their father's house. They began to run, rushed into the cottage, and fell into their father's arms.

The man had not had a single happy hour since he had left the children in the forest. The woman had died. Gretel shook out her apron so that the pearls and precious stones rolled about the room, and Hansel drew one handful after another from his pockets to add to them. Then all their troubles were at an end, and they lived together in complete happiness.

My tale is done, and there a mouse does run. Whoever catches it can make a big fur cap of it.

ISBN 0-590-44459-X

Copyright © 1988 by Neugebauer Press, Salzburg, Austria.
All rights reserved. Published by Scholastic Inc., 730 Broadway, New York, NY 10003, by arrangement with Picture Book Studio. BLUE RIBBON is a registered trademark of Scholastic Inc.

12 11 10 9 8 7 6 5 4 3 2 1   1 2 3 4 5 6/9

Printed in the U.S.A.   08

First Scholastic printing, August 1991